For my family and our camping missions

—K.G.

The Wishing Woods

Bibbidi Bobbidi Academy

Tatia and the Camping Trip Troubles

Written by Kallie George

Cover illustration and character design by

Lorena Alvarez Gómez

Interior illustrations by Andrea Boatta

DISNEP • HYPERION

Los Angeles   New York

First Edition, April 2024
1 3 5 7 9 10 8 6 4 2
FAC-073226-24039
Printed in the United States of America

This book is set in Superclarendon, Harman Elegant, Harman Sans/Fontspring.
Designed by Joann Hill
Illustrations created by Andrea Boatta and Lorena Alvarez Gómez

Library of Congress Control Number: 2023948699
ISBN 978-1-368-09880-9

Visit DisneyBooks.com

CHAPTER 1
Tatia Shine

Tatia Shine liked being first.

She was first to get up each morning at Bibbidi Bobbidi Academy, the school for fairy-godparents-in-training.

First to eat breakfast.

First to class and to finish her homework too.

But she wasn't first in her family to attend the Academy.

Her older sister had gone first,
and graduated too.

But now Tatia was about to do
something her sister *hadn't* done.

This week, the Academy was going on its very *first* camping trip in the Wishing Woods.

"A camping trip is a way to build relationships and have fun," said the Fairy Godmother, their headmistress. "Becoming a fairy godparent isn't all Bibbidi Bobbidi Boos. It's some yippee-yahoos too!"

Two of the teachers, Mr. Frog and Ms. Merryfeather, were coming. And the Fairy Godmother would visit for storytelling under the stars at the end. At the campsite, she said, you could see the brightest wishing star in the sky!

The camping trip was Tatia's chance to shine.

And she had *just* the thing to help her.

The Fairy Godmother Field Guide, written by the Fairy Godmother herself.

When Ms. Merryfeather asked who wanted to be in charge of it, Tatia's hand went up first.

Tatia checked it out from the Story Shed.

She chose the first edition.

The book was huge!

Tatia read through it once,
starting with the first page.

The book made her backpack so heavy, it was hard to flutter her wings.

But it didn't matter.

Last time Tatia was in the Wishing Woods, she had been a unicorn. Things hadn't gone exactly to plan.

But as long as she did everything by the book, this time things would go right. Tatia was determined.

She would make sure the school's first camping trip was a shining success!

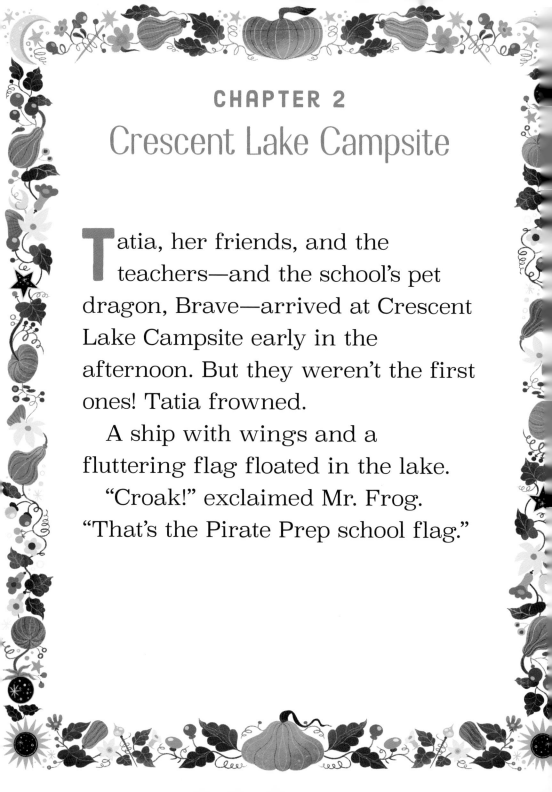

CHAPTER 2
Crescent Lake Campsite

Tatia, her friends, and the teachers—and the school's pet dragon, Brave—arrived at Crescent Lake Campsite early in the afternoon. But they weren't the first ones! Tatia frowned.

A ship with wings and a fluttering flag floated in the lake.

"Croak!" exclaimed Mr. Frog. "That's the Pirate Prep school flag."

"The fairy pirates must be camping here too," said Ms. Merryfeather.

Sure enough, the fairy pirates were set up right beside the Academy's campsite.

Pirate Prep was the school for fairy-pirates-in-training. While fairy godparents helped with wishes, fairy pirates learned how to help kids have adventures.

"Ahoy, mates!" came a call.

A teacher with two sparkly wings fluttered through the trees, wearing a large hat and big boots.

"Mr. McGilly!" croaked Mr. Frog. "Really—*ribbit*—nice to see you!"

As the teachers caught up, a
fairy-pirate-in-training waved
at Tatia and her friends. "Ahoy!"
She was wearing a large hat too,
and was carrying rolls of paper
under her arm. "I'm Briony Brigs,"
she said. "If you want to join our
activities, you can."

Tatia thought that sounded fun. But they needed to go by the book, and the book didn't say anything about joining fairy-pirate activities.

"Thank you," said Tatia. "Maybe later. We have a lot to do first."

"Jolly good!" Briony waved again and disappeared.

"Ooh, I can't wait! Fairy pirates are *full* of trouble," cackled Octavia, who used to be a sea-witch-in-training.

"Look, Mr. McGilly has already stolen away our teachers," whispered Ophelia.

That wasn't *quite* true. But Mr. Frog and Ms. Merryfeather *were* heading off with Mr. McGilly to set up their own site.

"We'll check in with you later," said Ms. Merryfeather. "Don't forget, blow your whistles if you need us."

Tatia's frown grew. So far, nothing was going like she expected.

But all she had to do was look in the book to get their perfect camping trip back on track.

She struggled to turn to the first chapter.

"'Make your site just right,'" read Tatia. "'Snug as a bug, cozy for a crew.'"

CHAPTER 3
Tent Trouble

Next door, the fairy pirates were already setting up their tents. Briony Brigs was directing them with a map.

"Come on, everyone," said Tatia. "Let's work together. One big tent for us all."

"The tent in the picture doesn't look crooked enough," said Octavia.

"It's not *supposed* to be crooked," said Tatia.

"I think it looks cozy," said Rory with a smile.

Tatia took out her wand.

Everyone else took out their wands too.

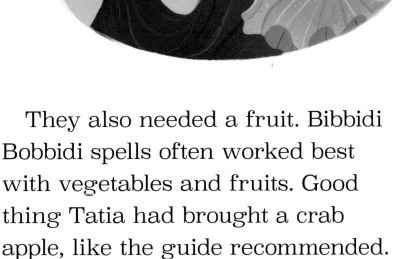

They also needed a fruit. Bibbidi Bobbidi spells often worked best with vegetables and fruits. Good thing Tatia had brought a crab apple, like the guide recommended. She pulled it out of her pocket.

"Bibbidi Bobbidi Boo!" they all said at the same time.

POOF!

A giant tent appeared in front
of them.

It had a bow on the top. Inside
were pillows and sleeping bags.

It DID look like the picture in the book . . . snug as a bug.

In fact . . . what was that?

Inch, inch, inch.

It *was* a bug! Actually, an insect. A caterpillar was crawling into their tent. Right onto a pillow.

"No, this is not the place for you," Tatia stated politely. But . . .

Scurry, scurry, scurry. Something else brushed past their legs.

It was a squirrel! It hopped into their tent and snuggled in.

"Stop!" said Tatia. "This is *our* tent." Rory and Mai started to laugh.

Rustle, rustle, rustle. In scurried a chipmunk, snuggling in beside the squirrel!

Now everyone was laughing— everyone except Tatia.

Their tent was by the book all right.

It was snug as a bug and cozy for a crew. A crew of critters.

Tatia couldn't believe it. The animals were even snoring!

She double-checked the book, but it didn't say what to do now.

"We'll have to make another tent," said Tatia. "But we don't have another apple! The guide said we only needed one."

"Don't worry," said Rory. "I don't need a spell to make a tent. I've made lots of forts. Maybe the fairy pirates can lend us some supplies."

"I'll come with you. That way we can carry more," said Mai.

"A fort? No, that's not what the book—" started Tatia.

Too late. Rory and Mai were gone.

Tatia grumbled.

Her stomach grumbled too.

She didn't want to leave their site all wrong. But . . .

"We will fix the tent later, when Rory and Mai get back," she said. "There are a lot of things we can still do."

And so Tatia turned to the next page of the enormous book.

TIME TO DINE, UNPACK YOUR SNACK

CHAPTER 4
Time to Dine

We need to make a campfire to cook some lunch," Tatia announced.

The book showed a picture of a campfire and hot dogs in fluffy, roly-poly rolls.

"Yum! We can roast marshmallows," cackled Octavia. "I just adooore sweets!"

Through the trees, they could see that Briony and the other fairy pirates were getting ready to make a fire too.

Some pirates were playing
sword-fight with the roasting
sticks. And . . . was that Mai and
Rory joining in?

Tatia frowned. She would have to
go get them. But first . . .

"We need to collect some sticks. *All* the sticks."

Tatia started, and her friends followed. They gathered sticks from around the trees. Under the bushes. Even near their packs.

Soon they had a big pile.

"Time to light the fire," said Tatia.

"Maybe Brave can light the fire," suggested Cyrus.

The little dragon looked hopeful.

A dragon-made fire *would* be special, but it wasn't in the book either.

"Sorry, Brave," said Tatia. "We are supposed to light it with our wands. But . . ."

Where WERE their wands?

Tatia looked. . . . Around the trees. Under the bushes. Even near their packs.

The wands weren't there.

They must be . . . "In the pile of sticks. Oh no!" cried Tatia.

"Oh *funny!*" Octavia laughed.

"I can help sort them," said Ophelia.

"No!" began Tatia. "I have to look in the book. . . ."

Too late.

Her friends were sorting.

Her friends were swishing and swooshing too! They were playing sword-fight with the sticks, like the fairy pirates.

"En garde, you sea pickle!" cried Octavia.

"Oops," said Octavia, sheepishly.
"We found the wands, Tatia."
"But now the sticks are *pickles*,"
Tatia moaned.

"And . . . where is Brave?" said
Cyrus.

They all looked up, just in time to
see Brave's blue tail disappearing
into the trees.

"He must be sad about not getting
to light the fire. I better go after
him," said Cyrus.

"I'll come help," said Ophelia.

"What about lunch?" said Tatia,
though she knew finding Brave
was more important.

Besides, Cyrus and Ophelia were already gone.

It was just Tatia and Octavia now. And a big pile of pickles.

But . . . Tatia didn't feel like eating a pickle. She didn't feel like eating anything. So far, the trip wasn't the shining success she had planned.

Maybe the next chapter of the book would change things. . . .

CHAPTER 5
Explore the Outdoors

E xplore the outdoors,'" Tatia read. "'Go for a swim, or a hike.'"

"Come on, Octavia," she said. "Time to swim. I'm sure when we are done, everyone will be back."

"Ooooh!" Octavia cackled. "How perfectly wicked! I adooore swimming."

Tatia put on her swimsuit and flitted with Octavia to the water's edge, not too far from the pirate ship.

Tatia carefully put the field guide on a rock, then stepped into the water.

Uh-oh!

Crescent Lake wasn't shaped like a full moon, but it WAS full.

Full of thick mud. Full of moon minnows. Full of reeds in rainbow colors. They were pretty but so slippery and squiggly. Yuck! The book hadn't prepared her for this.

Octavia splashed in.

Octavia loved the mess and the reeds and minnows and mud, but . . .

Tatia didn't feel like swimming here.

Yet, she had to follow the book. It was written by the Fairy Godmother herself!

So Tatia took another step into the water. . . . Ick!

"Yoo-hoo!" came a voice. "Would you like to join us on a treasure hunt?"

"Did someone say 'treasure'?" Octavia cackled, popping her head out of the water.

Briony Brigs was hovering above them.

"I'm just telling the teachers and getting a map," said Briony. "Your friends are coming. Would you like to come too?"

Briony Brigs seemed so nice. Except, a treasure hunt wasn't in the guide.

"No, we're going on a hike," said Tatia.

That was next in the book. But her voice wobbled.

"Actually," said Octavia, "I think I *will* go on the treasure hunt."

"Y-you . . . will?" Tatia stammered.

Nibble! A minnow nipped at her toe.

Tatia hopped out of the water.

"Fine!" She picked up the book, careful not to drip on it.

"Tatia, your swimsuit . . ." called Octavia.

Tatia wasn't listening. She was already on her way, hiking up, up, UP to the top of Star Point.

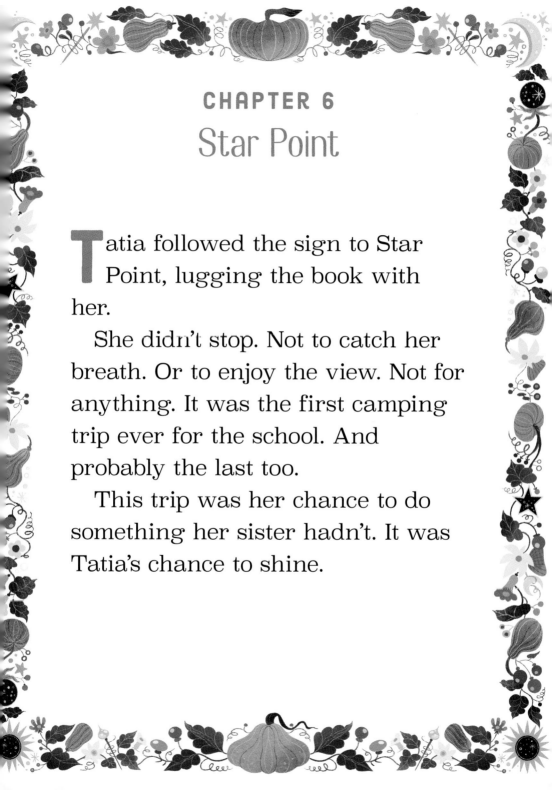

CHAPTER 6
Star Point

Tatia followed the sign to Star Point, lugging the book with her.

She didn't stop. Not to catch her breath. Or to enjoy the view. Not for anything. It was the first camping trip ever for the school. And probably the last too.

This trip was her chance to do something her sister hadn't. It was Tatia's chance to shine.

But nothing was going by the
book. If she hiked to the top like the
guide said—if she did at least *one*
thing right—maybe things would
turn around. They just *had* to!
Huff, huff. Puff, puff!

At last . . . she made it! Star Point!

Tatia was at the very top.

But she didn't feel happy. She just felt tired.

Tired and tearful.

The big book was so heavy.

She flopped down and opened it to the very last page.

Have fun with everyone.

Well, that was impossible! No one was here. The fairy pirates had stolen them away!

Tatia took a deep breath. No, that wasn't *quite* true.

Her friends had left for different reasons.

But maybe they weren't coming back because of her. She'd been trying so hard to do everything by the book, she'd forgotten to listen to her friends, and to her heart too. Even SHE wasn't having a good time anymore.

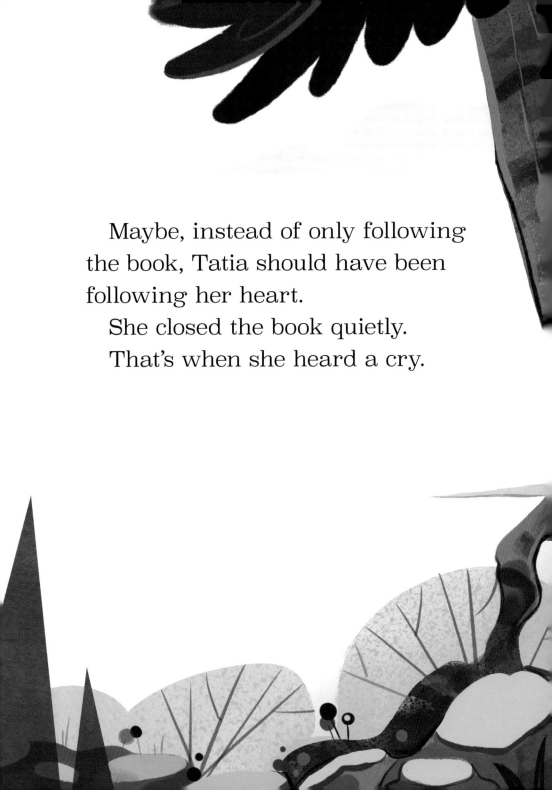

Maybe, instead of only following the book, Tatia should have been following her heart.

She closed the book quietly.

That's when she heard a cry.

CHAPTER 7
The Marshmallow Marsh

It was a cry for help. Tatia didn't need a book to know that.

The sound was coming from the trees.

Tatia quickly picked up the book and headed back down the path.

Before long, she reached the most magical part of the Wishing Woods, somewhere she'd never been.

It was a marsh—of *marshmallows*!

Big and little, pink, white, and
even blue!

And there, in the middle of the
marshmallow marsh, was Brave.

Cyrus fluttered off to the side.

So did Tatia's other friends and
the fairy pirates too.

Tatia was about to leap to the
rescue, when Cyrus said, "Stop!"

Tatia took a breath and listened.

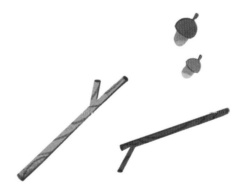

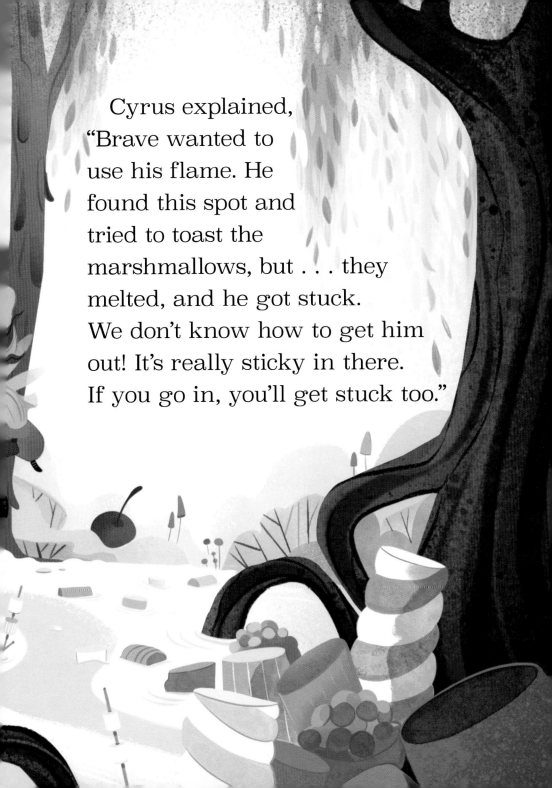

Cyrus explained, "Brave wanted to use his flame. He found this spot and tried to toast the marshmallows, but . . . they melted, and he got stuck. We don't know how to get him out! It's really sticky in there. If you go in, you'll get stuck too."

"Brave is scared," added Ophelia. "I'm so glad you are all here. We didn't want to leave him. And if we call for the teachers, this might be our last camping trip *ever*."

"Maybe the book can help?" Rory asked Tatia.

"I don't think so," said Tatia. "In fact, I'm certain it doesn't say anything about rescuing a dragon from a marshmallow marsh."

Briony Brigs looked worried.
"I don't have a map for this
either. I always follow a map for
everything."

A few of the other pirates rolled
their eyes.

"You do?" Tatia couldn't believe it.

Still, this time, she knew they
didn't need a map . . . or the book.

She looked around at her friends
and the fairy pirates.

They had everything they
needed right there.

CHAPTER 8
Unstuck

They had wooden swords to cut the strands of sticky marshmallow.

And . . . they had the book too!

It was so thick, it didn't get sucked into the marsh.

They could use it as a stepping stone to reach Brave.

Tatia set it in place.

Cyrus led the way, since he knew Brave the best. "It's okay, Brave," he said gently.

But they all worked together. And . . .

POP!

Brave was free!

"I'm sorry I didn't let you use your flame to light our campfire," said Tatia to the little dragon when he was safe.

Brave gave her a nuzzle.

He pressed his sticky snout against her cheek, and she closed her eyes and felt all warm inside.

She really felt like she was shining from the inside out.

It was growing darker now. It was time to go back to the campsite.

They still had the tent trouble to fix, and a campfire to make.

But it was so beautiful out, maybe they could just sleep under the stars.

CHAPTER 9
New Edition

Back at the campsite, the teachers were waiting for them. Not just the teachers, the Fairy Godmother too.

Tatia gulped. The critters were STILL snoring in the fairies' tent.

They didn't have a campfire going.

Not to mention she was still in her bathing suit!

The Fairy Godmother didn't look upset though. She was beaming.

"What a lovely idea to share your space! And you've explored the outdoors—I can tell by your face!"

"Yes, but . . . nothing went according to plan," stammered Tatia. "I'm so sorry. I tried to follow the book, but . . . it didn't work out."

"Sometimes things don't go according to plan," Mr. Frog croaked. "I used to be a frog before I was turned into a human. But I am happy to be a teacher now. If I were still a frog, I wouldn't have met all of you."

The Fairy Godmother smiled too. Then she looked down at the book. "Goodness me, what is that?"

"Oh, the field guide got a bit sticky," said Tatia, blushing. "I'll clean it off."

"Oh, no, my dear, I don't mean that. *That* edition is from long ago. I've updated it, didn't you know?"

"You did?" Tatia was surprised.

"Oh, my dear, I most certainly did. Fairy godparents learn and grow. Sometimes we follow a plan, and sometimes we go with the flow." She waved her wand. "Here."

Tatia expected an even BIGGER book. But to her surprise, the new field guide that appeared was smaller.

"This one is *much* improved. A book is grand to open your heart, but really it is just the start."

Tatia took the book and turned to the first page.

It WAS revised.

Because now the *first* part of the "Camping Trip" chapter read:

Have fun with everyone!

CHAPTER 10
Fun with Everyone

And that is just what Tatia did. After a bath, Brave lit a fire. The Academy and Pirate Prep combined their sites and made a big fort with sleeping bags and hammocks. They all roasted marshmallows (collected *carefully* from the marsh).

Most of all, Tatia talked with Briony. They had so much in common!

Briony dreamed of being a top fairy pirate and leading children in grand adventures. She had a fairy pirate sister who was older than her, just like Tatia. And she even had been transformed once herself—into a parrot!

Before bed, the Fairy Godmother pointed to the sky. "Can you see the brightest star?" she said. But no one could. Which one was it?

"That's exactly it," said the Fairy Godmother. "No single answer is right. It depends on who's looking and on which night."

Tatia looked up at the stars.

Wishes were being made around the world—and waiting to come true. She wondered what would happen next at their school, and with her friends. Maybe Briony could visit. Maybe she could visit Briony.

No matter what, it would be a first for her.

And Tatia couldn't wait.

Collect all the books in
the Bibbidi Bobbidi Academy series:

Rory and the Magical Mix-Ups

Mai and the Tricky Transformation

Ophelia and the Fairy Field Trip

Cyrus and the Dragon Disaster

*Tatia and the Camping Trip
Troubles*